WHO ATE STEVE?

For Arlo
S.L.

For Reuben and Nola
K.H.

First published 2024 by Nosy Crow Ltd
Wheat Wharf, 27a Shad Thames, London, SE1 2XZ, UK

Nosy Crow Eireann Ltd
44 Orchard Grove, Kenmare, Co Kerry, V93 FY22, Ireland

www.nosycrow.com

ISBN 978 1 83994 621 9 (HB)
ISBN 978 1 83994 622 6 (PB)

Nosy Crow and associated logos are trademarks and/or
registered trademarks of Nosy Crow Ltd.

Text © Susannah Lloyd 2024
Illustrations © Kate Hindley 2024

A CIP catalogue record for this book is available from the British Library.

Printed in China following rigorous ethical sourcing standards.

Papers used by Nosy Crow are made from wood grown in
sustainable forests.

10 9 8 7 6 5 4 3 2 1 (HB)
10 9 8 7 6 5 4 3 2 1 (PB)

WHO ATE STEVE?

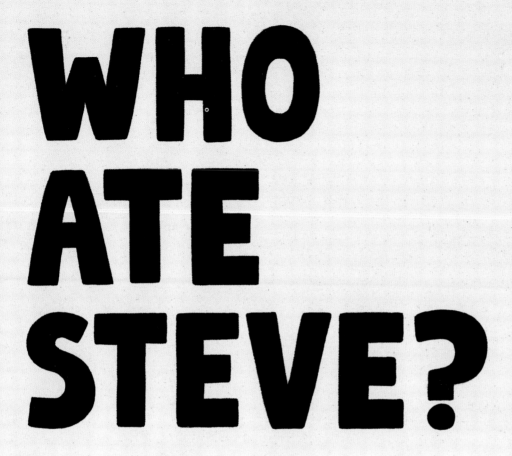

Written by Susannah Lloyd

Illustrated by Kate Hindley

nosy crow

Welcome, everyone, to this **EXTREMELY INTERESTING** book where we are going to learn all about

SIZE.

EXCITED?

I KNOW I AM!

First of all, we need some helpers . . .

MARCEL!

STEVE!

You'll do nicely.

Let's say thank you
to both of them.

THANK YOU, Marcel.
THANK YOU, Steve.

And off we go!

First, let us take a look at Marcel.

Now, Marcel, here, is

BIG.

Good. I think we've got that bit covered nicely.

GREAT STUFF!

So, Marcel is **BIG**,

but Steve is . . .

Wait a minute!
Where's Steve?

STEVE?

STEVE?!

Marcel?

Did you **EAT** Steve?

YOU DID, **DIDN'T YOU?!**
FOR SHAME, **MARCEL!**
SPIT HIM OUT
THIS INSTANT!

I'm waiting, Marcel.
We are **ALL** waiting.

We can't carry on with this
EXTREMELY INTERESTING book about **SIZE**
until you **RETURN STEVE.**

RIGHT NOW.

Thank you.

AND his
HAT,
if you please…

That wasn't so hard, was it?

Now, let's learn all about

SIZE!

So as I was saying,
Marcel, here, is

BIG,

but Steve,
on the other hand . . .

MARCEL!!!

THAT IS **NOT** THE SORT OF BEHAVIOUR WE EXPECT IN OUR BOOK.

I'M **NOT** GOING TO TELL YOU AGAIN, **MARCEL!**

YOU BRING **STEVE** BACK DOWN,

AT ONCE!

GOOD. Right.

Now, where was I?

Ah yes!
As I was saying . . .

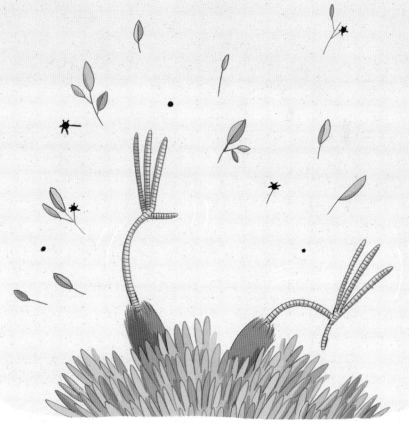

MARCEL . . .

I've got my eye on you . . .

OH, HOW DISAPPOINTING.
LOOK AT THE **CHILDREN**, **MARCEL**!
YOU ARE SPOILING THEIR LOVELY BOOK.
YOU ARE NOT **JUST** LETTING <u>YOURSELF</u> DOWN.

RIGHT.

Now, can we **PLEASE** behave ourselves
so that we can FINISH THIS BOOK?!
We've almost run out of pages!

SO, as I was saying . . .

MARCEL is **BIG**, and ...

STEVE is **SMALL**.

THERE! I've said it!

STEVE IS SMALL.

Well, that is **QUITE** enough for one day!

Thank you, Steve.
And thank **you**, Marcel.

Wait a minute!
Where's Marcel?

MARCEL?

MARCEL?!

FOR SHAME, FELICITY!

HOW COULD YOU?!